# *Dear Parent:*
## *Your child's love of reading starts here!*

Every child learns to read in a different way and at his or her own speed. Some go back and forth between reading levels and read favorite books again and again. Others read through each level in order. You can help your young reader improve and become more confident by encouraging his or her own interests and abilities. From books your child reads with you to the first books he or she reads alone, there are I Can Read Books for every stage of reading:

### SHARED READING
Basic language, word repetition, and whimsical illustrations, ideal for sharing with your emergent reader

### BEGINNING READING
Short sentences, familiar words, and simple concepts for children eager to read on their own

### READING WITH HELP
Engaging stories, longer sentences, and language play for developing readers

### READING ALONE
Complex plots, challenging vocabulary, and high-interest topics for the independent reader

### ADVANCED READING
Short paragraphs, chapters, and exciting themes for the perfect bridge to chapter books

I Can Read Books have introduced children to the joy of reading since 1957. Featuring award-winning authors and illustrators and a fabulous cast of beloved characters, I Can Read Books set the standard for beginning readers.

A lifetime of discovery begins with the magical words "I Can Read!"

*Visit www.icanread.com for information*
*on enriching your child's reading experience.*

*For Carolynn,*
*My Valentynn*
*—J. P.*

*For Alice, Matthew, Sarah, and Frannie*
*—M. H.*

HarperCollins®, ☝®, and I Can Read Book® are trademarks of HarperCollins Publishers.

Library of Congress Cataloging-in-Publication Data
Prelutsky, Jack.
It's Valentine's Day / by Jack Prelutsky ; pictures by Marylin Hafner.
    p.    cm. (I can read!)
"Greenwillow Books."
ISBN 978-0-06-053712-8 (trade bdg.) – ISBN 978-0-06-053714-2 (pbk.)
1. Valentine's Day—Juvenile poetry. 2. Children's poetry, American. I Hafner, Marylin. II. Title.
PS3566.R36I85 2009    2008022597    811'.54—dc22    CIP    AC

17 SCP  10 9 8 7 6 5    ❖    First Edition
Greenwillow Books

# I Can Read!

READING 3 ALONE

# IT'S VALENTINE'S DAY

BY JACK PRELUTSKY

PICTURES BY MARYLIN HAFNER

Greenwillow Books, *An Imprint of* HarperCollins*Publishers*

# Contents

# It's Valentine's Day

It's Valentine's Day,
and in the street
there's freezing rain,
and slush, and sleet,
the wind is fierce,
the skies are gray,
I don't think I'll
go out today.

But here inside,

the weather's warm,

there is no trace

of wind or storm,

and you just made

the morning shine—

you said you'd be

my valentine.

# A Valentine for My Teacher

My teacher's very special

so I'm making her a heart,

a valentine that's sure to be

a proper work of art.

I've worked on it all morning
so it should be ready soon,
I'd like to slip it on her desk
before this afternoon.

It's colored in with crayons
and it's trimmed with paper lace,
it has flowers, hearts, and cupids—
I can't *wait* to see her face.

# A Valentine for My Best Friend

You are rotten, you are crummy,

nasty, smelly, and a dummy,

you are absolutely awful,

and your breath should be unlawful.

You are ugly, you are simple,

and your brain is like a pimple,

you should soak your head in brine. . . .

WON'T YOU BE MY VALENTINE?

## Our Classroom Has a Mailbox

Our classroom has a mailbox
that we painted red and gold,
we stuffed it with more valentines
than it was made to hold.

When we opened it this morning
I was nervous as could be,
I wondered if a single one
had been addressed to me.

15

But when they'd been delivered

I felt twenty stories tall,

I got so many valentines

I couldn't hold them all.

## I Made My Dog a Valentine

I made my dog a valentine,

she sniffed it very hard,

then chewed on it a little while

and left it in the yard.

I made one for my parakeets,

a pretty paper heart,

they pulled it with their claws

and beaks

until it ripped apart.

I made one for my turtle,
all *he* did was get it wet,

I wonder if a valentine
is wasted on a pet.

# I Made
# a Giant Valentine

I made a giant valentine

to mail a special friend,

I'm sorry that I made it

for it's one I'll never send.

This morning at the playground
he was mean and made me sore,
and now I think I'm certain
I don't like him anymore.

He pelted me with snowballs,
*seven* hit me in the head,
I'm taking home that valentine
to give my cat instead.

## Oh No!

Oh no!

She kissed me on the cheek,

I'm so mad it's hard to speak,

that's a kiss I *must* erase.

Good-bye!

I'm off to wash my face.

# My Special Cake

It's Valentine's Day, so I'll create
a special cake to celebrate,
a cake as good as a cake can be
(I'm using my own recipe).

I dump some butter in a bowl,

add licorice as black as coal,

then jelly beans, and eggs, and rice,

and chocolate chips, a touch of spice.


I put in bits of peanut brittle,

salt and sugar (just a little),

flour too (a scoop or so),

and milk to help me mix the dough.


I drop in raisins (half a cup),

then stir and stir and stir it up.

The oven's on, the cake is in,

I'm wiping batter off my chin.

I hope my cake will turn out well. . . .

Wait! What is that awful smell?

It really doesn't look too nice,

I think I'll try a tiny slice.

Yuck! It has an awful taste,

like gluey gobs of smelly paste.

I wonder what I could have done. . . .

I'd better bake another one.

## There's Someone I Know

There's someone I know

whom I simply can't stand,

I wish he would bury

his head in the sand,

or move to the moon

or to deep outer space,

whenever I see him

I make a weird face.

28

Today during recess
outside in the yard,
he suddenly gave me
a valentine card.

I wish that he hadn't,

it made me upset,

it's the prettiest one

I could possibly get.

# Mother's Chocolate Valentine

I bought a box of chocolate hearts,

a present for my mother,

they looked so good I tasted one,

and then I tried another.

They both were so delicious

that I ate another four,

and then another couple,

and then half a dozen more.

I couldn't seem to stop myself,

I nibbled on and on,

before I knew what happened

all the chocolate hearts were gone.

I felt a little guilty,

I was stuffed down to my socks,

I ate my mother's valentine. . . .

I hope she likes the box.

# I Love You More Than Applesauce

I love you more than applesauce,

than peaches and a plum,

than chocolate hearts and cherry tarts

and berry bubble gum.

I love you more than lemonade
and seven-layer cakes,
than lollipops and candy drops
and thick vanilla shakes.

I love you more than marzipan,

than marmalade on toast,

oh, I love pies of any size,

but I love YOU the most.

# Jelly Jill Loves Weasel Will

Jelly Jill loves Weasel Will

and Will loves Flo the Fink,

Flo loves Tom Tomatoface

(at least, that's what I think).

Tom loves Steffie Sloppysocks

and she loves Pete the Punk,

Pete loves Gretchen Gumhead
and she loves Sam the Skunk.

Sam loves Linda Lemonmouth
and she loves Fred the Flea,
Fred's in love with Jelly Jill . . .

I wonder who loves me.

# My Father's Valentine

I'm working on a valentine,

my very special own design,

a heart to give my dad tonight

(it's quite a chore to get it right).

The first time that I cut it out,

one side was thin, the other stout,

and so I tried to fix it, but

I made an error when I cut.

I wasn't careful (though I tried),

and overcut the other side,

but one more snip should do it, then

whoops! I cut too much again.

A snip off here, a snip off there,

and maybe just another hair,

it's finally done, but understand

it's somewhat smaller than I'd planned.

It's not much bigger than a bean,

the tiniest heart I've ever seen,

I guess I'll give it to him now. . . .

I bet he likes it anyhow.

# I Only Got
# One Valentine

I only got one valentine,

and *that* was signed,

Love, Frankenstein.